Drew.

Puss in Boots

Other brilliant stories to collect:

Aesop's Fables
Malorie Blackman

The Six Swan Brothers
Adèle Geras

Hansel and Gretel
Henrietta Branford

The Seal Hunter
Tony Mitton

The Goose Girl
Gillian Cross

Cockadoodle-doo,
Mr Sultana!
Michael Morpurgo

The Snow Queen
Berlie Doherty

The Pied Piper
K M Peyton

The Twelve Dancing
Princesses
Anne Fine

Mossycoat
Philip Pullman

Grey Wolf, Prince Jack
and the Firebird
Alan Garner

Rapunzel
Jacqueline Wilson

Rumpelstiltskin
Kit Wright

The Three Heads in
the Well
Susan Gates

Puss in Boots

Retold by
Diana Wynne Jones

Illustrated by
Fanghorn

SCHOLASTIC
Home of the Story

Scholastic Children's Books,
Commonwealth House, 1–19 New Oxford Street,
London WC1A 1NU, UK
a division of Scholastic Ltd
London ~ New York ~ Toronto ~ Sydney ~ Auckland
Mexico City ~ New Delhi ~ Hong Kong

First published by Scholastic Ltd, 1999

Text copyright © Diana Wynne Jones, 1999
Illustrations © Fanghorn, 1999

ISBN 0 590 13422 1

All rights reserved

Printed by Cox and Wyman Ltd, Reading, Berks.

2 4 6 8 10 9 7 5 3 1

The right of Diana Wynne Jones and Fanghorn to be identified as the
author and illustrator respectively of this work has been asserted by
them in accordance with the Copyright, Designs and Patents Act, 1988.

Once there was a miller who had three sons. When he died, he left the mill to his eldest son. The second son got the donkey the miller used for carrying the sacks of grain and flour. But the youngest son got nothing but the black cat the miller kept to catch the rats and mice that lived in the cornbins.

The two elder sons were delighted. The second son left at once with his donkey. He went to live in the nearby town where the king lived, to start up in business as a carrier. The eldest son went on working the mill, which was doing so well that he was able to employ the youngest at quite a good wage. The youngest son was not

happy at all. Three days after his father's funeral, he sat sadly in the mill doorway with the cat on his knees and, although he told himself he was a grown man now and not a baby, a tear ran down his cheek, making a path in the flour there, and dropped on the cat's back. The cat looked up indignantly.

"Sorry, Puss," said the miller's son. He tried to brush the tear off and only succeeded in making a sticky white streak in the cat's black fur.

"Leave it," said the cat. "I can clean it off much better than you can.

What's the matter?"

"You *talk*!" said the miller's son.

"Of course," the cat replied. "But only when necessary. I asked you what was the matter."

The miller's son realized that what he had to say might offend the cat. He said very carefully, "It isn't that I don't value you, Puss. You're the best mouser in the country, and you're a great comfort when you sit on my knee and purr. But I think that my father didn't value me. He left both my brothers things that are worth a hundred times more than you are."

The cat was extremely offended. He drove all eight front claws into the young man's kneecaps but he answered quite calmly, "What do you know of value? Your father was a wise man. He knew that brains are worth more than ten mills and a hundred strong donkeys."

"I don't think I have any brains,"

the miller's son said sadly. "I shall be a miller's assistant all the days of my life. All I shall ever be is District Wrestling Champion."

"You're not that much of a fool," said the cat. "But it doesn't matter because I have brains enough for both of us. The question is, do *you* have brains enough to trust me and do exactly what I tell you to do?"

"I think so," said the miller's son. "I've always admired the cunning way you hunt."

"Good," said the cat. "Then your sorrows are over. Save up your money

until you can afford to buy me a pair of boots and a strong leather bag to match them."

"*Boots!*" said the miller's son. "Whatever for?"

"Uh-huh!" said the cat. "I said *trust* me. But if you must know, I get frustrated when I hunt out of doors. There are so many brambles."

"But whoever heard of a cat in boots!" said the miller's son.

"Precisely," said the cat. "People will sit up and take notice when they see me. Do it."

"All right," said the miller's son.

The mill was doing so well that year that it did not take the miller's son long to save the money. He

whistled as he hauled in sacks of grain and carried out sacks of flour, or when he helped his brother to adjust the vast wooden cogwheels of the mill's machinery, thinking that he was in good hands — or rather, paws. While he worked, the cat sat along the dusty rafters with his long tail hanging down, listening to the talk of the farmers and shop-keepers who came to bring grain and collect flour. The farmers talked of a fearsome ogre who had taken possession of all the lands to the east. The shopkeepers chattered

of the king's lovely daughter. She was old enough now to marry, they said, but she had refused every noble the king had found for her. The cat listened and then sat up and washed, thoughtfully.

At the end of May, the miller's son took his money, put the cat in a basket and walked into town to the shoemaker.

The shoemaker could not believe his ears.

"Boots?" he said. "Even if I could make a pair small enough, the beast would be miserable. It's unnatural. It's cruel."

At this, the cat put his head out of the basket. "No it's not," he said. "I asked for them."

The shoemaker swallowed and stared into the cat's green eyes. "Oh," he said at last. "Well, in that case, I suppose I... What colour does Your Worship wish your boots to be?"

"Red," said the cat. "And the bag the same. With a handsome fringe of course."

So the shoemaker measured the cat's hind feet and told the miller's son to come back for a fitting in two hours. The miller's son had just enough money left for a meat pie. He sat on the edge of the fountain in the market square while he waited, sharing the pie with the cat: the meat inside for the cat and piecrust for himself. As they were eating, a golden coach rattled by with

the Crown prince in it, most finely dressed, with his sister, the princess, sitting beside him.

"A splendid coach," the cat remarked.

"Her hair is just exactly the gold of wheat stalks," the miller's son replied, staring.

"And the prince's doublet has some very fine embroidery on it," the cat observed.

"Her eyes are like cornflowers," the miller's son answered. "Pure, pure blue."

The cat looked smug.

When they went back to the shoemaker, the boots were ready. The
shoemaker had used the softest
leather he had, for fear the cat would
be uncomfortable, and he had made
the boots beautifully, with fringed
tops to match the fringe on the bag.
He and the miller's son both expected
the cat to stumble about awkwardly in

them. But not a bit of it. The cat rose on his hind feet as if he were born to do that, looking somehow sleeker, taller and more impressive than before. He stamped a bit, twitched his tail and stalked round the shop. "These will do nicely," he said.

They returned to the mill with the cat striding ahead of the miller's son, sniffing at bushes and looking thoroughly pleased with himself. "Well, one of us is happy," said the miller's son. "What about me?"

"Give me a month," said the cat.

The next day the cat went hunting wearing his boots and carrying
the fringed bag. Joyfully, he crunched
through the brambles where the
thorns had formerly stopped him
going and, even more joyfully, he
stood in the bushes and watched the
fine fat rabbits feeding in the green
dell beyond, thinking themselves so

safe. He watched until two of the finest and fattest moved up beside the brambles. Then he pounced. *Wop!* That rabbit never knew what hit it. The second one knew and turned to run, but by this time the cat was on that one too. *Wop!* again. Two dead rabbits lay in the grass beside him.

The cat's mouth watered at the smell. But he was determined to keep faith with the miller's son who had trusted him. Besides, he could hunt for himself tomorrow. He sighed and stuffed both rabbits into the red fringed bag. Then heaving the bag on his shoulder, he strode off to the king's palace.

The cat knew the palace well. In his days as an ordinary mill cat he had often gone in there over the walls to sneak meat from the kitchens. He had fought stable cats there and kitchen cats, and pampered cats from the palace itself, all over the gardens and the roofs. He knew the place like the back of his paw. If his first plan did not work, he was prepared to go inside over the wall. But first he marched boldly up to the palace gates.

"Let me in!" he cried out. "I have a present for the king from the Marquis of Carabos."

The sentry at the gate was puzzled enough to ask the captain over. Both soldiers stared down at the small black upright figure in the handsome red boots. "What do you think?" murmured the sentry. "Should we let him in?"

"Well," said the captain, "I never heard of this Marquis of Carabos, but it's not everyone who has a cat in boots for their servant. Looks like a magic trick to me."

"You mean," asked the sentry, "this Carabos is a sorcerer of some kind?"

"I mean," said the captain, "that you don't want to offend sorcerers. The king would be mighty offended if we made him offend a sorcerer. But we'd cop it even worse if the stuff in that sack blew up in the king's face."

"I hear you," said the sentry. And he called out, "Hey, you! Puss in the

boots! Show us what's in that bag of yours before we let you in."

"A present from my master to the king," said the cat. "I told you." He dumped the fringed bag in the gateway and opened it to show the rabbits. "There. Freshly killed."

"Beautiful," said the captain, licking his lips. "Just leave them with us and we'll see they get to the king."

"I can't do that," said the cat, who had heard every word the soldiers had said to one another. "My master, the Marquis of Carabos, is the strongest sorcerer in the land and he ordered me

to give these rabbits to the king *myself*. Anyone who tries to stop me will of course become a frog. Perhaps I should have mentioned these facts straight away."

The sentry and the captain looked at one another. "Pass the puss in the boots, sentry," said the captain, and the sentry said woodenly, "Pass, Puss in Boots."

The cat stamped solemnly through, across the courtyard and on into the palace. Various courtiers and officials there tried to stop him, but he merely said, "A present to the king from my master, the Marquis of Carabos," and marched on. He arrived in the throneroom followed by quite a crowd of people, all anxiously wondering how magic he was and whether they should have stopped him.

The king was quite as astonished as the rest and exclaimed, "What have we here?"

The cat bowed, as graceful as only a cat can be. "Sire, I bring a present from my master, the Marquis of Carabos." He fetched the rabbits from his bag and held them out towards the king.

When he heard the cat speak, the king was convinced that the present must be from a master of magic and,

just like the soldiers, he was afraid of offending someone so powerful. He took the rabbits graciously. And they were very fine, he saw. "We thank your master for his kind present," he said. "And we shall certainly order them cooked for our supper."

"My master will be delighted to hear that," the cat said. He bowed again and marched out of the palace. Phew! he thought. So far, so good.

The next day, he caught a rabbit for himself and one for the mill while he was at it. "See," he told the miller's son, "I'm hard at work for you. Here is

your supper."

The day after that, the cat went hunting again, quite far afield, in the marshy borders of the ogre's lands, where he caught a bag full of fat ducklings which he carried to the palace.

This time, the sentry said straight away, "Pass, Puss in Boots."

"I thank you, my good man," the

cat replied, and he marched to the throneroom again. "A present from my master, the Marquis of Carabos," he told the king and he laid the ducklings on the steps of the throne. When the king looked up from admiring them, the cat had gone.

The cat hunted most days after that. Thanks to the boots, he was able

to go places he had never hunted before. Every other day, he brought the king something different: a brace of pheasants from the wide wheatlands beyond the marshes; a large hare from the uplands beyond those; quails from the cornfields; pigeons from the mill; fat marshbirds; live songbirds, which in those days were considered a truly royal present; and once, regrettably, a stray hen. This was on a day when it rained and hunting was difficult. Each time, he told the king it was a present from the Marquis of Carabos.

Everyone in the palace grew to expect him. They called him, like the sentry, Puss in Boots, and they all wondered very much about the master of such a servant and who the Marquis of Carabos was. But the cat, although he took care to linger around in the palace so that people could ask him, would say very little. "A great man," he told

the courtiers. "A kind and handsome master and an excellent landlord." This left the courtiers not much wiser.

The king was as curious as anyone, but he was very anxious not to offend the mysterious magician. It was not until nearly a month had passed, when the cat brought him the bag filled with succulent grouse, that he mustered the courage to ask, "My good cat, why does your master keep sending me these splendid presents?"

The cat was extremely relieved.

He had thought the king was never going to ask. "Because," he said, "the Marquis of Carabos wishes to be Your Majesty's friend."

"I am honoured," said the king. "But why does such an obviously powerful person wish for my friendship?"

"Naturally he does," the cat replied. "He is one of Your Majesty's subjects and your near neighbour as well."

"Is that so? Where does he live then?" the king asked, truly surprised.

"Why, in the castle to the east," the cat said, sounding quite as

surprised. "Surely Your Majesty knew that!"

"I had thought an og— No matter," said the king. He considered for a moment, and among his considerations was his daughter, the princess. "Since we are such near neighbours," he said at length, "would your master consent to visit me here in the palace?"

The cat bowed. "Sire, I will ask him."

He trotted off jubilantly home to the mill, where he took off his boots and passed the afternoon catching rats in the cornbins. "About time that lazy cat of yours did his job!" said the eldest brother.

"He does!" the miller's son protested. "He's not lazy. He brought us a hen yesterday."

"I'm pretty sure it was one of Mother Naismith's," said his brother.

"You ate it too," said the miller's son. He heaved up another sack of flour and went away with it before his brother could argue.

In the evening, the cat came out of the bins, washed carefully, put his boots on and went back to the palace, where he was hurried respectfully before the king. He bowed. "My master thanks you for your kind invitation, Sire," he said, "but he has an even better idea. He invites you, your family and the chief of your courtiers to come to dinner with him instead at

Castle Carabos. And he asks which day
would be convenient to Your Majesty."

"Tomorrow?" suggested the king,
who could by now hardly contain his
curiosity about the Marquis of Carabos.

The cat bowed again. "Tomorrow it
shall be, Sire. I will inform my master."

He strode out of the palace and
back to the mill. He arrived just as

work finished for the day and the miller's son took off his floury boots and apron and, with a weary sigh, sat down and put his feet up on a stool. The cat took off his boots too and hopped on to his master's floury knees. This was, to both their minds, the best part of the day. That day, however, instead of purring as usual, the cat said, "Ask your brother for the day off tomorrow."

"I can't!" said the miller's son. "We've got a load of oats to grind."

"I told you," said the cat, "to trust me and do as I say."

"But it means having a row with my brother," the miller's son objected.

"Yours is the choice," said the cat. "Tomorrow you can either stay as you are now for the rest of your life, or you can leave this life for ever in one way or another."

"All right, I'll ask," said the miller's son.

There was a lot of shouting in the mill that night and the cat kept prudently up in the rafters out of the way. In the morning, the miller's son said to him, "According to him, I'm a lazy good-for-nothing layabout with chaff for brains and he won't give me another day off until after midsummer, so this one had better be worth it. What do you want me to do?"

"Go and swim in the lake," said the cat. "You'll like that."

It was a hot day already, with that faint haze over the meadows that promises even more heat later. The

miller's son readily agreed to go bathing. He and the cat walked to the lake together, past fields, where people were already at work cutting grey swathes of hay, filling the air with the smell of moist grass. The miller's son smiled, in lazy delight. "This is a good idea," he said, when they reached the lake and saw it rippling, bleary blue beyond the rocks. "I'll swim from here."

"No," the cat said. "I want you on the other side, near the road from the palace."

The miller's son shrugged, but he walked on round the lake. The cat chose the place on the shore with great care. "Satisfied?" asked the miller's son, when he was at last allowed to undress.

"Yes," said the cat. "Now make sure you go right under. Get every trace of flour out of your hair as well as off the rest of you. It's important."

"But I could have done that in the millstream," the miller's son said,

holding his clothes suspiciously in front of him. "Why do it here?"

"You'll see. Go on in," said the cat. "I'll guard your clothes." He was keeping an anxious eye on the road above the shore. There was no one in sight on it yet, but he was beginning to want to scratch the miller's son. "Go on *in!*"

The miller's son shot him a last suspicious look and surged into the water. "Ouch!" he cried out. "It's icy!"

I *shall* scratch him, the cat thought. "If you don't swim," he

called out, "you'll be working in the mill for ever. Get *under*!"

Puffing, gasping and turning a raw mauvish colour, the miller's son did as he was told. As soon as he was far enough out and too busy gasping to notice, the cat snatched up the heap of floury clothes and dragged them out of sight under a heap of rocks. He was

just wedging the floury boots under too, when he heard the clatter of horses' hooves and the rilling of carriage wheels. He threw a rock on top of the clothes and hurried up on to the road.

When the king's procession rounded the corner, the cat was running backwards and forwards across the road shouting, "Help, help!"

The procession stopped. Everyone knew Puss in Boots. The king put
his head out of the golden coach and
asked what was the matter.

"My master!" yowled the cat.
"My master, the Marquis of Carabos,
is drowning in the lake!"

The king snapped out orders.
The soldiers with him jumped off
their horses and rushed down to
the lake, where the miller's son was
throwing up great spouts of water
in his efforts to keep warm. The
Crown prince rushed after them,
followed by a crowd of courtiers,

followed more slowly by the king and the princess. They were in time to see the miller's son being hauled to the shore and looking mighty astonished about it. He looked even more astonished when the captain of the soldiers said to him, "Was your lordship unable to save yourself by magic?" and probably might have made an unwise answer, had not the captain seen the princess coming and hastily thrown his cloak around the miller's son.

"Thanks — but you needn't," gasped the miller's son. "My clothes are over there — Oh!"

"Robbers have stolen the clothes of my master, the Marquis of Carabos!" promptly yowled the cat. "What shall we do?"

"Don't worry, Marquis," said the Crown prince. "You seem to be

about my size. Let me send a servant
back to the palace for some of my
clothes."

First someone assumed he could
do magic, and now everyone thought
he was a marquis. The miller's son
shot the cat a worried look. "That's
very good of you," he stammered.

"Indeed it is," the cat put in.
"My master, the Marquis of
Carabos, is eternally obliged to Your
Highness. And while you wait for
the clothes, I shall run on ahead and
warn the servants at the castle that
you are on your way."

The miller's son knew as well as anyone that the castle belonged to an ogre. He shot the cat a look of pure horror. The cat ignored it and went trotting away along the road, thoroughly pleased with the way things were going so far. As soon as he was out of sight of the coaches, he put on speed and fair galloped. In a very short time, he arrived at the lush lands by

the river where he had caught the
ducklings for the king. The grass here
was several times thicker and greener
than the lands by the lake. A herd of
beautiful Jersey cows grazed up to
their udders in it in one field, while
the field next to the road was being cut
for hay. The haymakers, astonished to
see a cat in red fringed boots, stopped
work and crowded to the fence to
stare.

"Look your fill," the cat told them. "I am only a messenger. The king is on his way behind me. When he passes, you must tell him that these grasslands belong to the Marquis of Carabos."

"But we can't do that!" the farmer objected. "These meadows belong to the ogre."

"And a cruel rent he charges," added the farmer's wife.

"Nevertheless," the cat said coldly, "you must tell the king that the Marquis of Carabos owns them. The ogre wishes it. If you don't, he'll come and eat you."

They turned pale and agreed at once.

The cat left them and galloped on. The road now wound into the higher lands where the cat had caught pheasants for the king among the growing sweetcorn. The land was rich here too. The corn stood two metres high, while in the fields beyond the wheat stood green with full heads and barley waved silver and lusty. Here, the farmer and his sons were working with mattocks on a blocked ditch by the side of the road, and they all turned to stare at a cat in boots.

The cat stopped and stared back. "The king is coming," he said. "If he asks you whose lands these are, you must say they belong to the Marquis of Carabos."

"But they belong to the ogre," the farmer protested.

"The ogre wants you to tell the king that they belong to the Marquis of Carabos," the cat said, staring green

and fierce. "If you don't, he will eat
your eldest son and double your rent."

The farmer went grey with fear.
"Very well," he agreed.

"Mind you do," said the cat, and
galloped on, further uphill to the
uplands where he had caught the
grouse and the hare for the king, until
he came to a place where he could see

the ogre's castle at the top of its hill.
There, where the turf was thick and
sweet, sheep with long white fleece
were grazing the hillside and beside
the road was a large paddock full of
splendid thoroughbred horses. The
people in the paddock tending the
horses turned to look at the cat and
shook all over at the sight.

"More of his enchantments," they
whispered to one another. "Does he
want to eat us, or just the horses?"

"On the contrary," the cat said to
them. "I come from the good and
great Marquis of Carabos, who is on

his way here with the king. When the king arrives, you must tell him these sheep and these horses all belong to the Marquis of Carabos."

"But," whispered the head groom, "they belong to..." and he did not finish the sentence. He simply pointed his thumb at the castle above.

"My master, the Marquis of Carabos, promises," said the cat, "that if you tell the king these animals belong to him, he will rid you of the ogre for good. But only if you make sure to tell the king that they belong to the marquis."

The grooms exchanged looks. "We'd do anything," said one. "All right. We'll tell the king."

"Good," said the cat, and went on up to the castle.

Meanwhile, the miller's son stood shivering by the lake, wondering when he would be executed for fraud and tried not to stare at the princess.

The princess, for her part, could not take her eyes off him. She had never seen a young man with such muscles, nor with such an open, honest look. And when at length a servant came galloping back from the palace with a bundle of the Crown prince's clothes, and then led the miller's son behind some rocks — where he respectfully helped him dress — the princess discovered this young man was even better looking than she had supposed. His hair was drying reddish brown — her favourite colour. And she there and then resolved to marry

him. What was the use of having the king for one's father, if not for just this?

"Father," she said.

"One moment, my love," said the king. "Marquis, since the robbers seem to have stolen your horse too, perhaps you would accept a seat in our coach?"

"My pleasure," stammered the miller's son.

So the procession moved off again, with the miller's son sitting beside the Crown prince and opposite the king. "Marquis, we can now thank you personally for all your gifts," the king said.

"My pleasure," the miller's son said again, and wished the cat had told him what he had been up to.

"Father —" began the princess.

But the Crown prince, who had also noticed the miller's son's muscles, said at the same moment, "Do you wrestle by any chance, Marquis?"

"Yes, from time to time," the miller's son admitted. "When I get the chance."

"I love to watch wrestling," said the Crown prince. "I shall never forget the contest between the miller's two younger sons last midsummer. Did you happen to see it?"

The miller's son was sure the Crown prince was showing him that he at least knew he was a fraud. "I saw

some of it," he admitted. "But I was rather occupied at the time."

"You should have seen it all," said the Crown prince. And he went on to describe — in great detail and with huge enthusias — every hold and throw in that contest.

"Father —" interrupted the princess.

"Just a moment, my dear." The king rapped on the roof to stop the coach and pushed down the window. "Those are wonderful cattle out there! And the best crop of hay I've ever seen! Here, my good man!" he called to the farmer. "Who is it who owns

this marvellous land?"

"Er – ah – the Marquis of Carabos, Your Majesty," came the reply.

The miller's son felt his face going red. He began to hope he would get the chance to strangle that cat before the king hanged him.

"Splendid!" the king said and they drove on. The Crown prince

went back to describing the wrestling, and the princess sighed.

Shortly, they passed the place where the farmer and his sons were working in the ditch. The king once more stopped the coach and asked whose land this was. "Oh, the Marquis of Carabos, to be sure, Sire," the farmer's eldest son replied swiftly.

"Wonderful!" exclaimed the king as the coach drove on. "My dear Marquis, I have seldom seen such heads on wheat or such well-grown

corn, and as for the barley, I'm amazed. I really do congratulate you."

What with this, and expecting the Crown prince at any moment to recognize him as one of the wrestlers, and trying not to meet the blue, blue eyes of the princess, the miller's son scarcely knew where to look. He felt even worse when the coach mounted the

hill and came abreast of the paddock full of thoroughbred horses. Here the grooms were so eager to make sure that they did as the cat had told them that they came rushing into the road almost before the coach had stopped.

"Sire!" shouted one. "You will wish to know that these fine horses all belong to the Marquis of Carabos."

"And the sheep. And the sheep too, Your Majesty!" clamoured the others.

"Extraordinary," said the king,

while the miller's son looked up at the castle and simply hoped the ogre would kill them all quickly.

The cat had reached the castle by then. He had never dared enter the castle before this day, but this did not stop him climbing the steep steps to the massive door, where the first thing

that met his nose was the delicious scent of the ogre's dinner cooking. Good. He boldly entered the huge hall beyond, which was quite clean and well kept apart from a pile of huge bones in the huge hearth. Good again. The ogre himself was sitting at the vast table. Not so good. He was a medium-sized ogre, greyish and covered with warts and blotches, with the most impressive fangs. The cat – who owned impressive teeth himself, except they were about a hundred times smaller – shook in his boots at the sight of those long white fangs.

But he advanced as boldly as he had entered the castle, while the ogre, like everyone else, stared at the sight of a cat in boots.

"What do you want?" rumbled the ogre. "Speak up before I munch you up and spit out your boots. I happen to need my dinner."

The cat bowed. "Curiosity killed

the cat, they say," he said. "I heard a silly story in town, Lord Ogre, and I had to come and ask you if it is true. You can't *really* turn yourself into any animal you want to, can you?"

"Silly story?" the ogre boomed irritably. "Of course it's true. If I wanted to, I could turn myself into a lion and eat you up. As it is, I shall just eat you."

The cat bowed again. "Forgive me, Lord Ogre. Before you eat me, can you *show* me how you can turn into something else? I find it very hard to believe you can be anything any bigger than you are."

"Show you?" yelled the ogre. "You miserable, disbelieving little runt! I'll show you all right!" And he stood up, still yelling, and swelled and swelled. His grey skin became grey scales, his fangs doubled in size and number in his ever-lengthening mouth, his yells became roaring and his hands and

feet grew enormous talons. Finally, a vast grey tail shot out behind him and lashed the flagstones. "Now do you believe?" he roared, advancing on the cat.

The cat dashed for shelter under the table, while this thing like a great grey dragon went crawling and roaring round it, trying to flick its tongue

out long enough to catch the cat as he dodged.

"Just a second, Lord Ogre," the cat called, peeping round a table leg. "One other question before you eat me. Can you do small as well as large?"

"What do you mean?" thundered the vast grey dragon-thing.

"Then you can't," the cat said, pretending to be disappointed. "It's easy to swell up, but you can't turn yourself into anything you have to shrink to be."

"Can't?" bellowed the dragon-thing. "Can't *shrink*? What do you think I can't shrink into?"

"Something *really* small?" said the cat. "Like – like a mouse?" As he said this, he quietly slid out of his boots. This had to go right and he could not risk his back legs slipping.

"I can so!" howled the dragon-ogre.

"Watch this!" And he began to shrink. He shrank and he dwindled and he shrank again – from barn-size, to house-size, to shed-size, and then to table-size and to dog-size – and by then, his grey back had grown humped and his eyes were like two large beads behind his pointed, twitching nose, and his tail was like a length of rope.

The cat grew still, as only a cat can be. His eyes stared at the shrinking thing like two green moons. His hind legs gathered up gently beneath him and just the very end of his tail

twitched while he measured the distance. And he waited. And the dog-sized ogre shrank to cat-size and then smaller still, until its tail was like a short piece of string. Then he grew whiskers. At last, a little grey mouse ran towards the table, squeaking, "There! I can so be a mouse!"

The cat's answer was *Wop!* Crunch! The mouse never even saw him spring. And to be on the safe side, he ate the ogre up entirely, tail, whiskers and all. Then he sat up and put on his boots, after which he stalked out from under the table to find all the ogre's human

servants crowded in the doorways in frightened huddles.

"Look lively there," the cat told them. "The king is arriving now to have dinner here. Some of you clear away those bones and the rest of you get the table ready and bring the food. Tell the kitchens there'll be at least forty people coming."

By this time, the king was coming slowly up the steps with the princess holding his arm and everyone else following behind. The cat hastened to the great doorway and bowed. "Welcome to Castle Carabos, Your Majesty."

At this, the miller's son leaned anxiously around the king. "Is ... everything in order? I mean, is dinner prepared?" he asked rather desperately.

"Certainly, my Lord Marquis," the cat purred. "They're just bringing the food in now." And he ushered everyone into the hall.

"How splendidly huge!" the king said, staring around it. If there ever had been an ogre, he decided, then this clever young Marquis of Carabos had destroyed that ogre by magic.

The princess pulled his sleeve. "Father," she said, "whether you like it or not, I want to marry the Marquis of Carabos. Now."

"It's odd you should say that, my dear," said the king. "I was just

thinking something on the same lines myself. That is, I hope you have no objection, Marquis?"

"Not at all," said the miller's son. "My pleasure." After that, he and the princess could not seem to take their eyes off one another – either then, or during the lavish dinner that followed – and scarcely found time to eat.

Everyone else ate heartily, because as it turned out, dinner for one ogre was enough to feed forty humans. The only one who ate nothing at all was the cat.

"What's the matter?" the miller's son asked him.

"Nothing," said the cat. "A touch of indigestion, perhaps. Master, if I can claim a reward, may I ask that no one ever makes me catch a mouse again?"

"Certainly," said the miller's son, who was just beginning to realize that he had somehow actually become the Marquis of Carabos, and that he

owned lands and a castle and was
going to marry a truly beautiful
princess, and that he owed it all to his
cat. "You shall live on trout and duck
and chicken for the rest of your days,"
he told the cat. "You've earned it."

And so it was.

Other stories to collect:

Aesop's Fables

Malorie Blackman

Illustrated by Patrice Aggs

Once upon a time there was a man named Aesop
who told stories full of wisdom...

Hansel and Gretel

Henrietta Branford

Illustrated by Lesley Harker

Once upon a time there were a brother and sister
who were left alone in the forest...

The Snow Queen

Berlie Doherty
Illustrated by Siân Bailey

Once upon a time there was a little boy whose
heart was turned to ice...

The Twelve
Dancing Princesses

Anne Fine
Illustrated by Debi Gliori

Once upon a time there were twelve princesses,
and no one knew why their shoes were full
of holes...

Grey Wolf, Prince Jack and the Firebird

Alan Garner

Illustrated by James Mayhew

Once upon a time there was a prince who set out
to seek the mysterious firebird...

Mossycoat

Philip Pullman

Illustrated by Peter Bailey

Once upon a time there was a beautiful girl whose
mother made her a magical, mossy coat...

The Six Swan Brothers

Adèle Geras
Illustrated by Ian Beck

Once upon a time there was a brave princess
who saw her six brothers turned into swans...

The Three Heads in the Well

Susan Gates
Illustrated by Sue Heap

Once upon a time there were two stepsisters —
one good, one bad — who both went out to seek
their fortunes...

Cockadoodle-doo, Mr Sultana!

Michael Morpurgo
Illustrated by Michael Foreman

Once upon a time there was a rich and greedy
sultan who met a clever little cockerel…

Rapunzel

Jacqueline Wilson
Illustrated by Nick Sharratt

Once upon a time there was a baby who was
stolen by a witch…

Rumpelstiltskin

Kit Wright

Illustrated by Ted Dewan

Once upon a time there was a beautiful girl who would die if she couldn't spin straw into gold…

The Goose Girl

Gillian Cross

Illustrated by Jason Cockcroft

Once upon a time there was a princess who lost everything she had ever owned…

The Pied Piper

K M Peyton

Illustrated by Victor Ambrus

Once upon a time there was a town infested
with a plague of horrible rats...